To
Rydek

I Spotted A Spotted Giraffe

Written By
Keith Lawrence Roman

Morningside Books

Illustrated By Barbara Litwiniec

I Spotted A Spotted Giraffe
Morningside Books Hardcover Edition
Copyright © 2016 Keith Lawrence Roman
All rights reserved.
Published in the United States of America by
Morningside Books, Orlando, Florida

This edition is cataloged as:
ISBN 978-1-945044-03-8
MorningsideBooks.net

Printed in China

I Spotted A Spotted Giraffe

Near to my house there is a park, where until dark I play.
I sometimes wear a funny hat, my costume for the day.
I might become a fireman or driver in a race.
One day I am a cowboy, the next day I'm in space.

Regardless of the hat I wear, I'm ready to explore
Any great adventure that I find outside my door.
Usually I carry, binoculars to view,
Many wild creatures I might capture for the zoo.

As daylight ends the landscape tends to shift and seems to change.
The shadows melt into the ground to blend and rearrange...

While walking in the jungle I spotted a spotted giraffe.
His neck was long and his tongue was purple,
I thought I heard him laugh.
He saw that I was watching and ran across a field,
Headed for the forest, the trees to be his shield.

I quickly took off after him and tried to match his stride.
With legs so long and powerful he swiftly left my side.

I tracked him by his tracks into the forest green.
Surely all those cocoa spots would stand out and be seen.
But tall and brown as he might be, I could not find him there.
Instead I found a monkey with dark brown blackish hair.
That ape was not afraid of me, but something made him scare.

Next time I'll bring a camera and soon all will remark
That after noon when shadows shade and melt into the dark,
Giraffes can still be spotted, hiding in the park.

About The Author

Keith Lawrence Roman has been writing stories of all kinds since he was seven years old. He has written over twenty different children's books, in several different styles.

Keith's favorite books from his childhood were Mike Mulligan and his Steam Shovel, Horton Hears a Who, Harold's Purple Crayon and every book ever written by Beverly Cleary.

His most popular books are rhyming children's picture books like the best-selling I Sat Beside An Elephant.

Yet his personal favorites among his books are young adult novels such as The Midget Green Swamp Moose, fairy tales like The White Handkerchief and chapter books for children 8 years old and up.

Keith was raised in a small town on the North shore of Long Island, New York. He considers himself an original baby boomer and a true child of the 60s.

He vividly remembers standing in snow every winter day, with near frozen toes waiting, for an always late school bus.

Keith takes great pride in that "somehow all those beautiful ideals we believed in from 1968 are still intact within me."

Keith speaks one on one with thousands of children every year and reminds them that, as Dr. Seuss said, "There's nobody youer than you."

His advice for writers both young and old is the same.

"First, make sure you are madly in love with your idea for a story. Much of writing is boring drudgery. Your idea must be strong enough to keep your inspiration alive while you write the story. Second, Do not paint only the branches of the writing tree, paint every leaf with all its color. And finally, don't wait until you are 57 to publish your first book. Let nothing in life frighten or distract you from expressing your thoughts."

Keith currently lives in Orlando, Florida where his feet are never too cold.

He screamed and screeched in Chimpanese
and climbed onto a tree.
Whatever had just frightened him, by now had frightened me.

I looked into the deeper woods inside that darkest lair.
Someone or some other thing let loose a glaring stare.
What was in there watching me? A leopard or a bear?

My head and palms were pooled with sweat.
My heart beat hard from fright.
Looking west, then looking east, I walked into the night.

I had no gun, no knife or net to capture any beast.
Those eyes had been so evil, a tiger at the least.
Would I subdue the danger there, or be the creature's feast?

Suddenly he darted forth up to the highest limb.
Walking slowly to the north I soon would capture him.
I gathered all my courage, needing to be brave.
As frightened as I was, I think, that he was more afraid.
I'd treed him in a tree it seemed. I heard the branches break,
As he jumped about the leaves, leaving with a shake.
What type of tiger is it there that flees into a tree?
How could a fearless tiger be so afraid of me?

That night while on safari the sun too quickly fell.
I couldn't find my way back home, the darkness hid the trail.
The trees had all surrounded me somewhere in the park.
One never should go wandering in Africa after dark.

Instantly the earth was lit from lights set high on poles.
A dozen small electric suns released a brilliant glow.

All the darkness disappeared, the park was set ablaze.
Everything was clearly seen, no longer in a haze.

The danger that I thought was there was leaves caught in a whirl.
The tiger it turned out to be, was just a tiny squirrel.
The monkey was a Pekinese, a puppy overwrought.
He barked and seemed extremely pleased, he also had been lost.
But I was sure, and I still am, there was a tall giraffe.
He wasn't just a playground slide, I know, I heard him laugh.

His purple tongue was not a flag, his spots were cocoa brown.
I didn't just imagine him, from shadows on the ground.

I realize hidden by the night that many things can hide.
But something big as a giraffe can never be disguised.